Text copyright © 2015 by Harriet Ziefert
Illustrations copyright © 2015 by Sophie Fatus
All rights reserved / CIP data is available.
Published in the United States by
🍎 Blue Apple Books
515 Valley Street, Maplewood, NJ 07040
www.blueapplebooks.com

Printed in China 04/16
ISBN: 978-1-60905-524-0
3 5 7 9 10 8 6 4 2

Can You Whoo, Too?

by Harriet Ziefert   illustrations by Sophie Fatus

BLUE APPLE

Do cows MOO all the time?

A cow will only moo to tell
other cows that it is time
to eat, to find other cows
if she finds herself alone,
or if she cannot see her calf.
Why do you think these cows
are mooing?

Why does a cow not sound
like you? She cannot do
anything but moo because
her lips do not move very
much. Try keeping your lips
still when you say, "cows moo."

Cows moo.

How about you?

Owls hoot-whoo.

When do owls HOOT?

There are clues in this picture that tell you what time of day you will most likely hear an owl.

Hoots tell other owls to stay away or to come close. A hoot will say, "stay away" because that owl wants all the mice in the woods to himself! A hoot will say "come close" when it is time to make a new owl family.

Can you hoot, too?

Whales sing songs.

Can you sing along?

Why do whales SING?

Male humpbacks compose beautiful music because females like it. Listen to their songs online and see if you like it!

While humpbacks sing, all whales make clicks, whistles, and pulses to "talk" with one another. Clicks also help whales find their way in the ocean. The sound of a click will hit an object in the water and bounce back to the whale. That bounce tells a whale the shape and distance of things in front of her—like food!

Monkeys cheep.

What are monkeys saying?

There are over 260 different kinds of monkeys, and they all use sounds to say what they are feeling. Just like you, a monkey will help others by making a sound that says, "watch out!" when danger is near.

Can you cheep?

Sheep bleat.

Can you bleat?

How do lambs find their dam?

A lamb knows his mother, or "dam," by the sound of her bleat. If you closed your eyes, could you find your favorite person just by the sound of his or her voice?

Lions roar.

Can you roar
even more?

Why do lions ROAR?

Every night a lion will roar
to tell other lions where he is.
The roar is like a fence to tell
other lions to "stay out."
Lions only want to share
their food with others in
their pride, or family.

Roars even help lions
get that food! An antelope
that hears a roar knows he
is in danger. If a roar is
very close, an antelope may
freeze in terror rather than
keep running.

Do you think a lion can
catch an antelope that
is standing still?

Why is the barnyard noisy?

Barnyards are made up of all sorts of animals saying, "get out of my way," "look out!," and "food!" in their own way.

Roosters will crow when something in their day changes. They will crow when night turns to day, when a tractor's motor starts, or something gets too close to the rooster or the hens.

A gosling will talk to his goose parent from inside the egg! Those goslings will grow up to honk when they are happy, afraid, or want other geese to follow them. Pigs speak to other pigs with oinks and grunts.

What do you think they say to one another with those sounds?

Roosters cock-a-doodle-do.
Can you cock-a-doodle-do, too?

Ducks quack.
Can you quack, too?

Do pigs oink? Yes, they do!

It's a squawk
for a hawk.

Deer are silent.
They don't talk.

You can talk.
But can you squawk?

How quiet is a deer?

All animals use their sounds and their bodies to tell others about food and danger. Deer do make grunts, sniffs, barks, and bellows, but they are quieter than many other animals.

A deer can tell other deer things by flicking her tail, twitching her ears, stomping her feet, and making other movements. The squirrels running through the trees above the deer flick their bushy tails when danger is near.

How do you say things with your body and not your voice?

Honk goes the goose.

Honk goes the moose.

What do HONKS say?

A honk by a male moose tells a female that he is looking to start a family. If the female agrees, she will respond with a long bawling sound. Outside of this conversation each fall, a moose is very quiet. One may come out of the woods and give you a big, tall surprise.

A goose's honk from the front of a flying flock says, "follow me!"

Do you know what season it is when geese fly south?

Which honk is the goose?
Which is the moose?

What do you hear in a corral?

Horses have a lot to say to other horses and to humans. A neigh says, "I'm looking for someone," and a nicker is the greeting when that someone appears.

Donkeys do not like to be alone and will bray with gusto when another donkey or human appears. If a human is late with a donkey's supper, his bray can say, "Hurry up, I'm hungry!"

Most of the sounds a mouse makes cannot be heard by humans. The squeak we do hear says, "I'm scared." A mouse's happy sound is a clicking or chittering that comes from snapping her teeth.

Horses neigh.

onkeys bray.

Mice squeak.
Eek! Eek!